It Jes' Happened

When Bill Traylor Started to Draw

by Don Tate

illustrated by R. Gregory Christie

Lee & Low Books Inc. • New York

ACKNOWLEDGMENTS

First, I thank God. Second, I thank my friends of the Austin chapter of SCBWI (Society of Children's Book Writers and Illustrators): Dianna Hutts Aston, Cynthia Leitich Smith, Chris Barton, Anne Bustard, and many others. I couldn't have done this without their support and encouragement.

Thank you to Lee & Low Books for recognizing new voices, and to my editor, Louise May, for patience, wisdom, professionalism, and support.
—D.T.

AUTHOR'S NOTE

This story is true to the facts of Bill Traylor's life and the times during which he lived, although there are discrepancies among sources about some dates and aspects of his life. In crafting this biography, I relied on the most authentic sources available, my knowledge of the communities in which Traylor lived, and the realities of society at the time.

The quote "It jes' come to me" on page 5 has long been linked to Bill Traylor, said to be a response he gave when a reporter, Allen Rankin, asked Traylor why he began to draw. Charles Shannon, Traylor's friend and supporter, later said Traylor never replied to the question and that Rankin put the words in Traylor's mouth, adapting them from something Shannon himself had said to Rankin.

AUTHOR'S SOURCES

Helfenstein, Josef, and Roman Kurzmeyer, eds. *Bill Traylor 1854–1949: Deep Blues.* New Haven, CT: Yale University Press, 1999.

Johnson, Sarah. "Unearthing the 'Deep Blues': How Bill Traylor's folk art was discovered and preserved for generations." *Austin American-Statesman,* August 15, 1999, Lifestyle section: K6.

Karlins, Nancy. "Bill Traylor." *Raw Vision,* no. 15 (Summer 1996): 28–35.

Kucera, Greg. "Bill Traylor: Works on Paper." Greg Kucera Gallery, Inc. http://www.gregkucera.com/traylor.htm.

"Learn About the Artists: Bill Traylor 1854–1949 American." The Anthony Petullo Collection of SELF-TAUGHT & OUTSIDER ART. http://www.petulloartcollection.org/the_collection/about_the_artists/artist.cfm?a_id=56.

Lyons, Mary E. *Deep Blues: Bill Traylor, Self-Taught Artist.* New York: Charles Scribner's Sons, 1994.

Rankin, Allen. "He Lost 10,000 Years." *Collier's* 117, no. 25 (June 22, 1946): 67.

Sobel, Mechal. *Painting a Hidden Life: The Art of Bill Traylor.* Baton Rouge: Louisiana State University Press, 2009.

QUOTATION SOURCES

p. 5: "It jes' . . . me." Quoted in Allen Rankin, "He Lost 10,000 Years," *Collier's* (June 22, 1946), 67.

p. 11: "You could . . . of money," "but you . . . it." Quoted in Mary E. Lyons, *Deep Blues: Bill Traylor, Self-Taught Artist* (New York: Charles Scribner's Sons, 1994), 13.

p. 12: "Minute he . . . his mama." Quoted in Phil Patton, "High Singing Blue," in Josef Helfenstein and Roman Kurzmeyer, *Bill Traylor 1854–1949: Deep Blues* (New Haven, CT: Yale University Press, 1999), 110.

p. 17: "My white . . . scattered." Quoted in Roman Kurzmeyer, "The Life and Times of Bill Traylor (1854–1949)," in Helfenstein and Kurzmeyer, 172.

p. 29: "I wanted . . . man plowing." Ibid.

"Bird on . . . know it." Quoted in Phil Patton, "High Singing Blue," in Helfenstein and Kurzmeyer, 110.

"Sometimes . . . need 'em." Quoted in Alfred M. Fischer, "Looking at Bill Traylor: Observations on the Reception of his Work," in Helfenstein and Kurzmeyer, 163.

p. 31: "This ole . . . his life." Quoted in Allen Rankin, "He Lost 10,000 Years," *Collier's,* 67. Spelling adapted.

LEE & LOW BOOKS Inc., 95 Madison Avenue, New York, NY 10016
leeandlow.com
Manufactured in China by Toppan, February 2012
Book design by Christy Hale
Book production by The Kids at Our House
The text is set in P22 Stanyan
The illustrations are rendered in acrylic and gouache
10 9 8 7 6 5 4 3 2 1
First Edition

Library of Congress Cataloging-in-Publication Data
Tate, Don.
It jes' happened : when Bill Traylor started to draw / by Don Tate ; illustrated by R. Gregory Christie. — 1st ed.
p. cm.
Summary: "A biography of twentieth-century African American folk artist Bill Traylor, a former slave who at the age of eighty-five began to draw pictures based on his memories and observations of rural and urban life in Alabama. Includes an afterword, author's note, and sources"—Provided by publisher.
ISBN 978-1-60060-260-3 (hardcover : alk. paper)
1. Traylor, Bill, 1854–1949—Juvenile literature. 2. African American painters—United States—Biography—Juvenile literature. 3. Folk artists—United States—Biography—Juvenile literature. 4. Alabama—Biography—Juvenile literature. I. Christie, R. Gregory. II. Title.
ND237.T617T38 2012
759.13—dc23   [B]   2011035353

For Tammy, my wonderful wife,
whose love inspires me to dream big dreams —*D.T.*

For Sue McGuire, it has always been nice —*R.G.C.*

It was early summer in Montgomery, Alabama, 1939. On downtown Monroe Avenue, an elderly man sat on a wooden crate. With a board laid across his lap and the stub of a pencil grasped in his hand, he began to draw a picture on the back of a discarded laundry soap box.

Who was this man, and what caused him to start drawing at the age of eighty-five? His name was Bill Traylor, and if people had asked him, he might have said, "It jes' come to me."

Back in the 1850s, George Hartwell Traylor and his wife owned a cotton farm near Benton, Alabama. The Traylors also owned more than twenty slaves. Sometime during 1854, one of the enslaved families had a baby boy. He was given the name Bill. His last name became Traylor, the same as his masters'.

From the minute the sun lit the sky until it disappeared into the night, the slaves picked cotton in the hot, dusty fields. When Bill was old enough, he was put to work too: pulling weeds, fetching water, gathering wood.

After he finished his chores, Bill sometimes met his friends at the bank of the Alabama River. They jumped into the cool water and waved at the steamboats passing by.

Without realizing it, Bill saved up memories of these times deep inside himself.

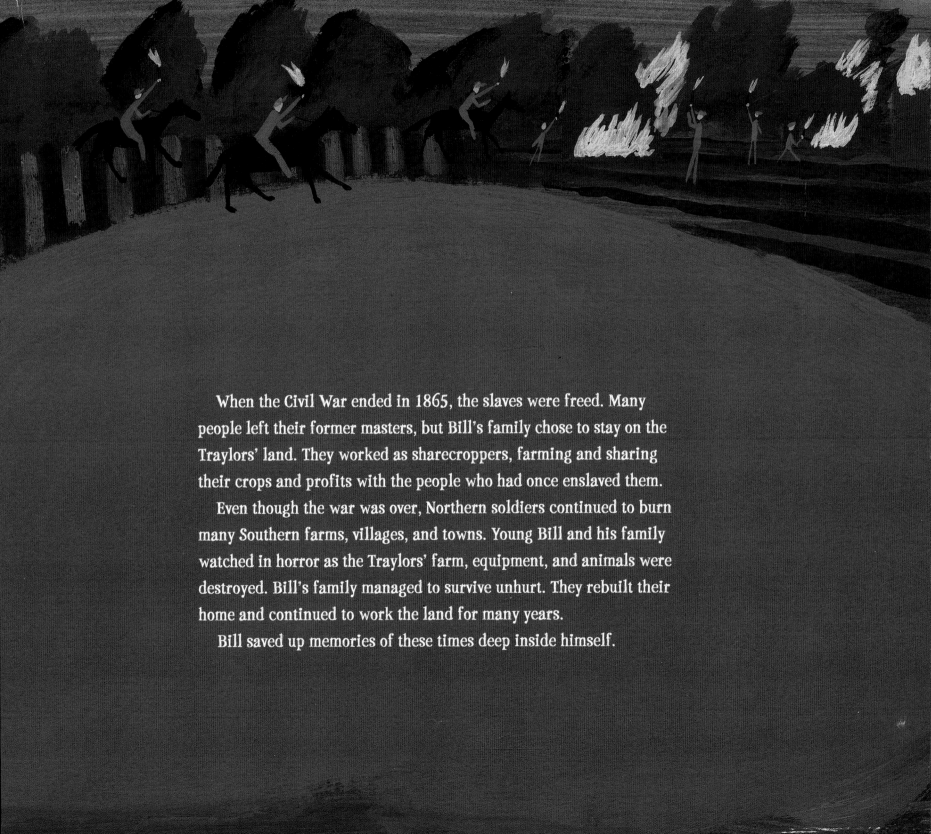

When the Civil War ended in 1865, the slaves were freed. Many people left their former masters, but Bill's family chose to stay on the Traylors' land. They worked as sharecroppers, farming and sharing their crops and profits with the people who had once enslaved them.

Even though the war was over, Northern soldiers continued to burn many Southern farms, villages, and towns. Young Bill and his family watched in horror as the Traylors' farm, equipment, and animals were destroyed. Bill's family managed to survive unhurt. They rebuilt their home and continued to work the land for many years.

Bill saved up memories of these times deep inside himself.

By 1881 Bill was a grown man, a hardworking farmer. He married a young woman named Lorisa, and they lived in a small cabin by a creek. Soon their home was filled with a brood of hungry children.

Money was scarce. "You could have that building over there full of money," Bill once said, "but you couldn't eat it." So everyone—even the littlest child—worked on the farm to grow the food they needed to fill their empty bellies.

Bill saved up memories of these times deep inside.

Bill had many animals, including a mule that helped him complete his chores.
But sometimes that mule turned stubborn when Bill approached with his plow.
"Minute he sees a plow he start swinging back. . . . Git's dat pride from his
mama," Bill said, annoyed that the mule refused to work.

The animals on the farm also amused Bill. He chuckled as he watched them go
about their business. Chickens strutted in the yard with confidence. Cats tiptoed
across rooftops with grace. Snakes slithered through brush, always up to no
good. Some animals even had personalities that reminded Bill of people he knew.

Bill saved up these memories deep inside.

Come Saturday night the men danced to the tune of a fiddle while the women sang up a storm. Children ran back and forth, snapping their fingers to the beat of the music. Even owls in the trees bobbed their heads to the music.

After the festivities the men took their dogs and went hunting and fishing until late into the night. The next day Bill roasted sweet potatoes and whatever he had caught and served them up for dinner.

Sunday morning folks gathered alongside the riverbank.
Under the shade of tall trees, they formed a circle around
the preacher and listened to his message in song. With praises
of joy, they clapped and raised their hands to the sky.
Bill saved up these memories deep inside.

Bill spent a lifetime on the Traylors' land. By 1935 he was eighty-one years old, way up in age and all by himself. "My white folks had died and my children scattered," Bill said. His wife had died too. With the people he was close to gone, Bill had no reason to stay on the farm. He packed his bag and headed to the nearby city of Montgomery.

Finding a job in the city wasn't easy. Bill had never learned to read or write, and his work on the farm hadn't prepared him for city life. Eventually he found employment at a shoe factory. But Bill developed painful rheumatism in his joints. Before long he was forced to quit his job.

For a while Bill sold pencils provided to him by the U.S. government. He didn't make much money, and he soon became homeless. During the day he wandered through downtown Montgomery. It was an exciting place to be. People bustled along, going in and out of markets, shops, and restaurants. Automobiles and horse-drawn buggies rumbled through the streets.

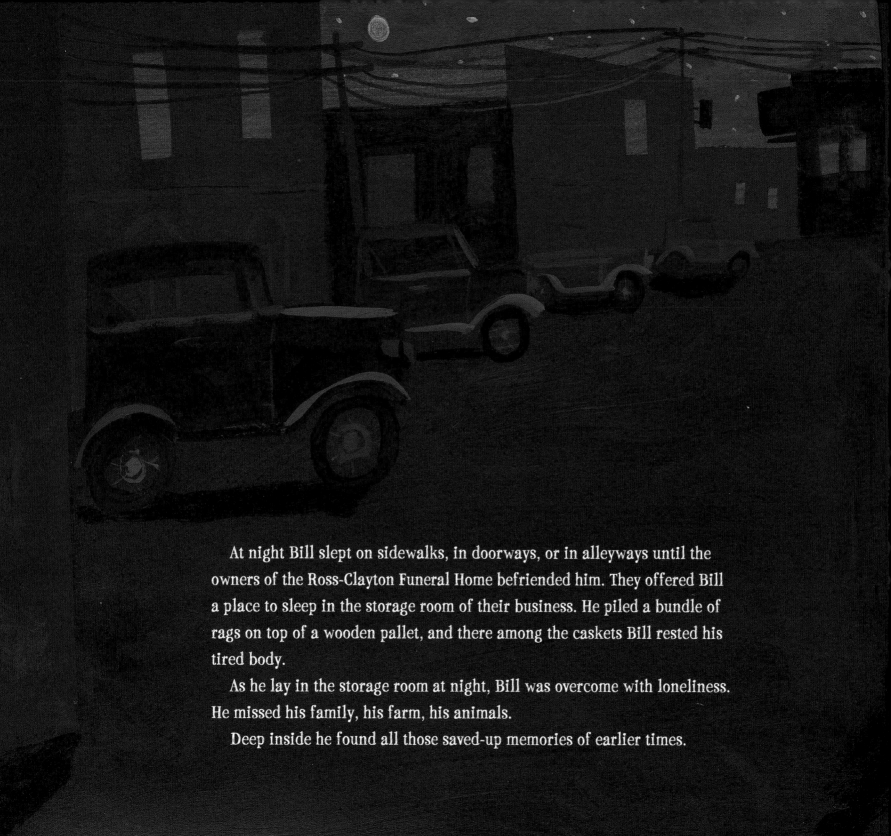

At night Bill slept on sidewalks, in doorways, or in alleyways until the owners of the Ross-Clayton Funeral Home befriended him. They offered Bill a place to sleep in the storage room of their business. He piled a bundle of rags on top of a wooden pallet, and there among the caskets Bill rested his tired body.

As he lay in the storage room at night, Bill was overcome with loneliness. He missed his family, his farm, his animals.

Deep inside he found all those saved-up memories of earlier times.

Bill could not contain his memories. One day in early 1939 he picked up the stub of a pencil and a piece of discarded paper and began to pour out his memories in pictures. Bill's first drawings were simple items: cats, cups, shoes, baskets. Then he began to draw human and animal forms too. He used the side of a stick to rule straight lines and shapes. Rectangles became bodies. Circles became heads and eyes. Lines became outstretched arms, hands, and legs. He filled in shapes with sketchy lines and smoothed out edges.

The sidewalk of Monroe Avenue became Bill's art studio. A wooden crate was his artist's bench. Scrap cardboard and old paper cartons were the canvases on which he drew his pictures. And the *clang-clang-clang* from the nearby blacksmith's shop provided background music for Bill while he worked.

Folks of all ages came to watch Bill work. One of his admirers taught Bill to write his name. Soon he was proudly signing his drawings.

Bill often hung his pictures on a nearby fence. When passersby asked questions about his drawings, Bill didn't mind. He could be quite talkative. But if Bill was focused on his work, he offered no conversation at all.

On a summer morning in 1939, a young artist named Charles Shannon caught sight of Bill sitting on his crate, drawing. Charles was intrigued as he watched Bill's hand make its marks, then fill them in. Bill's pictures danced with rhythm unlike any drawings Charles had seen.

Charles began visiting Bill regularly and wanted to support his work. He brought Bill art supplies: colored pencils and paintbrushes, poster paints and high-quality paper. But Bill liked to do things his own way. He used the colored pencils and some of the paints, but he continued to work on the backs of discarded bags, signs, and cardboard boxes.

Bill's hands were steady and confident. He was not concerned about messing up, and he almost never erased. When painting, he favored a rich, spare palette of colors: deep blues, bright reds, sunny yellows, and earth browns. He used paint straight from the jar and rarely mixed colors together.

Soon Bill moved to a shady spot on North Lawrence Street. There he continued to pour out his memories, often drawing until late in the day. He drew wide-eyed owls, a big red dog, and fighting cats. He sketched spotted snakes and hunters on horseback.

Sometimes Bill talked about his pictures. "I wanted to be plowing so bad today, I draw'd me a man plowing," he said. "Bird on top of the basket and he don't know it," Bill joked about one of his humorous pictures.

Bill also drew the people he saw on the streets of Montgomery: men in tall hats and women in patterned dresses, folks walking dogs and a man with a crutch. He drew the blacksmith's shop and blacksmithing tools arranged in rows.

When people paid him a few cents for one of his pictures, Bill was amused. "Sometimes they buys 'em when they don't even need 'em," he remarked.

Charles Shannon so admired Bill's work that he arranged for a show of Bill's drawings and paintings. The exhibit, *Bill Traylor—People's Artist*, was held at the New South art gallery on February 12, 1940. About one hundred of Bill's works hung on the walls of the gallery.

Bill moved slowly from picture to picture without saying much. Finally he pointed his cane at one of the paintings and said, "This ole horse, he fat, but this poor ole skinny mule here, he done work all-l-l-l his life."

None of Bill's art sold that day, but that didn't bother Bill. Money was not the motivation behind his drawings. Bill drew pictures for himself, to enjoy the saved-up memories of his life. He didn't know his pictures would also bring enjoyment to others. But without realizing it, Bill Traylor shared his memories with the world.

Afterword

Bill Traylor at work on Monroe Avenue, ca. 1940; photo by Jean and George Lewis

It was reported that when Bill Traylor visited the exhibit of his work at the New South art gallery, he walked around the room and occasionally commented on the artwork as though he had never seen any of it before. After Traylor returned to North Lawrence Street, he never mentioned the exhibition again.

Charles Shannon (1914–1996) was born in Montgomery, Alabama. He studied at the Cleveland School of Art, and while there he became interested in painting the culture of the South, especially that of African Americans. After moving back to Alabama, Shannon met Bill Traylor in 1939, and within a couple of weeks began bringing him art supplies. Over the next three years Traylor created somewhere between 1,200 and 1,500 drawings and paintings. Shannon continued to support Traylor by purchasing many of his works.

Shannon arranged for a second exhibit of Traylor's drawings at the Fieldston School of the Ethical Culture in Riverdale, New York, in January 1942. The Museum of Modern Art in New York City attempted to purchase sixteen drawings from the exhibition, but Shannon rejected the museum's offer of only one or two dollars per piece.

In June 1942 Shannon was drafted into the military, where he served until 1946. During that time Traylor drifted among the homes of various relatives throughout the country. The rheumatism in his left leg became worse, which led to gangrene and then amputation. After his wound healed, Traylor went back to his spot on North Lawrence Street.

By the time Shannon returned to Montgomery, Traylor's health had deteriorated even more. Traylor had left his place on the street and was living with one of his daughters in another part of the city. Disheartened and uninspired, Traylor continued to draw, but his pictures lost their spark. He died in October 1949 at the age of ninety-five.

For many years Charles Shannon kept Bill Traylor's art in storage because of a lack of public interest. By the late 1970s Shannon decided it was time to share Traylor's drawings with the art world again. As a result, in 1982 Traylor's work was exhibited at the Corcoran Gallery of Art in Washington, D.C. The exhibition, entitled *Black Folk Art in America 1930–1980*, included thirty-six of Traylor's pictures and led to wide recognition of his work. Since then Bill Traylor has come to be regarded as one of the most important self-taught American folk artists of the twentieth century. His pictures are also considered to be "outsider art," work created by a person without formal training who lives on the edge of established culture and society and works outside the mainstream art world of schools, galleries, and museums.

Exactly why Bill Traylor started to draw remains a mystery. Perhaps the ability to draw was within him his entire life, surfacing when circumstances made it possible. Whatever the reason, on a city sidewalk far away from his rural home, Bill Traylor re-created his life with imagination, humor, and engaging simplicity.

Bill Traylor. Blue Man with Umbrella and Suitcase, 1939

The Nursery Rhymes of Winnie the Pooh

A Classic Disney Treasury

Disney
PRESS

NEW YORK

Printed in the United States of America.
Based on the Pooh stories by A. A. Milne (copyright The Pooh Properties Trust).

5 7 9 10 8 6 4

Library of Congress Catalog Card Number: 98-84080

ISBN: 0-7868-3178-2

The Nursery Rhymes of
Winnie the Pooh

Table of Contents

A-Hunting We Will Go

A-hunting we will go,
a-hunting we will go.
Hi, ho, the merry-o,
a-hunting we will go.

Are You Sleeping?

Are you sleeping, are you sleeping,
Brother John, Brother John?
Morning bells are ringing,
Morning bells are ringing.
Ding, ding, dong.
Ding, ding, dong.

Baa Baa Black Sheep

Baa baa black sheep, have you any wool?

Yes, sir, yes, sir, three bags full.

One for my master, one for the dame,

And one for the little boy who lives down the lane.

Bye Baby Bunting

Bye baby bunting,

Father's gone a-hunting

To catch a little rabbit skin

To put bye baby bunting in.

13

Clap, Clap, Clap Your Hands

Clap, clap, clap your hands,

Clap your hands together.

Clap, clap, clap your hands,

Clap your hands right now.

Did You Ever See a Laddie?

Did you ever see a laddie,

a laddie, a laddie?

Did you ever see a laddie

go this way and that?

Go this way and that way,

go this way and that way.

Did you ever see a laddie

go this way and that?

The Farmer in the Dell

The farmer in the dell, the farmer in the dell,

Hi, ho, the derry-o, the farmer in the dell.

The farmer takes a wife, the farmer takes a wife,

Hi, ho, the derry-o, the farmer takes a wife.

The wife takes a child, the wife takes a child,

Hi, ho, the derry-o, the wife takes a child.

The child takes a nurse, the child takes a nurse,

Hi, ho, the derry-o, the child takes a nurse.

The nurse takes a dog, the nurse takes a dog,

Hi, ho, the derry-o, the nurse takes a dog.

The dog takes a cat, the dog takes a cat,

Hi, ho, the derry-o, the dog takes a cat.

The cat takes a mouse, the cat takes a mouse,

Hi, ho, the derry-o, the cat takes a mouse.

The mouse takes the cheese, the mouse takes the cheese,

Hi, ho, the derry-o, the mouse takes the cheese.

The cheese stands alone, the cheese stands alone,

Hi, ho, the derry-o, the cheese stands alone.

Head and Shoulders, Knees and Toes

Head and shoulders, knees and toes, knees and toes.

Head and shoulders, knees and toes, knees and toes.

Eyes and ears and mouth and nose.

Head and shoulders, knees and toes, knees and toes.

Here We Go 'Round the Mulberry Bush

Here we go 'round the mulberry bush,
the mulberry bush, the mulberry bush.
Here we go 'round the mulberry bush,
so early in the morning.

Hey Diddle Diddle

Hey diddle diddle,

the cat and the fiddle.

The cow jumped over the moon.

24

The little dog laughed to see such a sight,

And the dish ran away with the spoon.

Hickory, Dickory, Dock

Hickory, dickory, dock!
The mouse ran up the clock.
The clock struck one,
The mouse ran down,
Hickory, dickory, dock!

27

Hush, Little Baby

Hush, little baby, don't say a word,

Momma's gonna buy you a mockingbird.

If that mockingbird won't sing,

Momma's gonna buy you a diamond ring.

If that diamond ring turns brass,

Momma's gonna buy you a looking glass.

If that looking glass gets broke,

Momma's gonna buy you a billy goat.

If that billy goat won't pull,

Momma's gonna buy you a cart and bull.

If that cart and bull turn over,

Momma's gonna buy you a dog named Rover.

If that dog named Rover won't bark,

Momma's gonna buy you a horse and cart.

If that horse and cart fall down,

you'll still be the sweetest little baby in town.

I Am Walking

I am walking, walking, walking,

I am walking, walking, walking,

I am walking, walking, walking,

I am walking, walking, walking,

Now I stop.

I'm a Little Teapot

I'm a little teapot, short and stout.

Here is my handle, here is my spout.

When I get all steamed up, hear me shout,

"Just tip me over and pour me out."

If You're Happy and You Know It

If you're happy and you know it,
clap your hands.

Clap, clap.

If you're happy and you know it,
clap your hands.

Clap, clap.

If you're happy and you know it,
Then your face will surely show it.
If you're happy and you know it,
clap your hands.

Clap, clap.

If you're happy and you know it,
stamp your feet.

Stamp, stamp.

If you're happy and you know it,
stamp your feet.

Stamp, stamp.

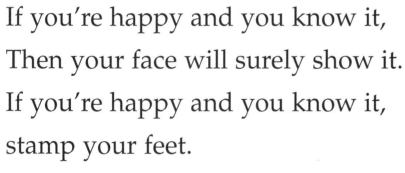

If you're happy and you know it,
Then your face will surely show it.
If you're happy and you know it,
stamp your feet.

Stamp, stamp.

If you're happy and you know it,
nod your head.

Nod, nod.

If you're happy and you know it,
nod your head.

Nod, nod

If you're happy and you know it,
Then your face will surely show it.
If you're happy and you know it,
nod your head.

Nod, nod.

If you're happy and you know it,
pat your knees.

Pat , pat.

If you're happy and you know it,
pat your knees.

Pat , pat.

If you're happy and you know it,
Then your face will surely show it.
If you're happy and you know it,
pat your knees.

Pat , pat.

In a Cabin, in the Woods

In a cabin, in the woods,

Little old man by the window stood.

Saw a rabbit hopping by,

Knocking at his door.

"Help me, help me!" the rabbit said,

"Or the hunter will catch me instead!"

Little rabbit, come inside;

Safely you'll abide.

It's Raining, It's Pouring

It's raining, it's pouring,

The old man is snoring.

He went to bed

And bumped his head,

And didn't wake up till morning.

The Itsy-Bitsy Spider

The itsy-bitsy spider went up the water spout.

Down came the rain
and washed the spider out.

Out came the sun
and dried up all the rain.
And the itsy-bitsy spider
went up the spout again.

41

Jack and Jill

Jack and Jill went up the hill
To fetch a pail of water.
Jack fell down and broke his crown,
And Jill came tumbling after.

Jack Be Nimble

Jack be nimble,

Jack be quick,

Jack jump over the candlestick.

Ladybug, Ladybug, Fly Away Home

Ladybug, ladybug, fly away home.

Your house is on fire, your children are gone.

All except one, her name is Nan.

She crept under a frying pan.

Lazy Mary

Lazy Mary, will you get up,

Will you get up,

Will you get up?

Lazy Mary, will you get up,

Will you get up this

morning?

Little Duckie Duddle

Little Duckie Duddle

Went wading in a puddle,

Went wading in a puddle quite small.

Said he, "It doesn't matter

How much I splash and splatter,

I'm only a duckie, after all. Quack, quack."

Little Green Frog

Ah—ump, went the little green frog one day.

Ah—ump, went the little green frog.

Ah—ump, went the little green frog one day.

And his green eyes went *blink, blink, blink.*

Little Jack Horner

Little Jack Horner sat in a corner,

Eating his Christmas pie.

He stuck in his thumb and pulled out a plum,

And said, "What a good boy am I."

London Bridge

London Bridge is falling down, falling down,
  falling down,
London Bridge is falling down, my fair lady.
Take the key and lock him up, lock him up,
  lock him up,
Take the key and lock him up, my fair lady.

Mary Had a Little Lamb

Mary had a little lamb,

Little lamb, little lamb,

Mary had a little lamb

Whose fleece was white as snow.

Everywhere that Mary went,

Mary went, Mary went,

Everywhere that Mary went

The lamb was sure to go.

It followed her to school one day,

School one day, school one day.

It followed her to school one day,

Which was against the rules.

It made the children laugh and play,

Laugh and play, laugh and play.

It made the children laugh and play

To see a lamb at school.

Mary, Mary, Quite Contrary

Mary, Mary, quite contrary,
How does your garden grow?

"With silver bells and cockle shells
And pretty maids all in a row."

Miss Mary Mack

Miss Mary Mack, Mack, Mack,

All dressed in black, black, black,

With silver buttons, buttons, buttons,

All down her back, back, back.

She asked her mother, mother, mother,

For fifteen cents, cents, cents,

To see the elephant, elephant, elephant,

Jump over the fence, fence, fence.

He jumped so high, high, high,

He touched the sky, sky, sky,

And didn't come back, back, back,

Until the Fourth of July, -ly, -ly.

Miss Polly Had a Dolly

Miss Polly had a dolly that was
    sick, sick, sick,
So she telephoned the doctor to come
    quick, quick, quick.
The doctor came with her bag and her cap.
And she knocked on the door with a
    rat-a-tat-tat.
She looked at the dolly and she shook her head.
"Miss Polly, put that dolly straight to
    bed, bed, bed."
She wrote on the paper for the
    pill, pill, pill,
"I'll be back tomorrow with the
    bill, bill, bill!"

Muffin Man

Do you know the muffin man,
the muffin man,
the muffin man?
Do you know the muffin man
who lives on Drury Lane?
Yes I know the muffin man,
the muffin man,
the muffin man.
Yes I know the muffin man,
who lives on Drury lane.

Oats, Peas, Beans

Oats, peas, beans, and barley grow;

Oats, peas, beans, and barley grow;

Do you or I or anyone know

How oats, peas, beans, and barley grow?

Old King Cole

Old King Cole was a merry old soul,

And a merry old soul was he.

He called for his pipe and he called for his bowl,

And he called for his fiddlers three.

Old MacDonald

Old MacDonald had a farm,
   E-I-E-I-O.
And on his farm he had a pig,
   E-I-E-I-O.
With an oink oink here
And an oink oink there
Here an oink, there an oink,
Everywhere an oink oink,
Old MacDonald had a farm,
   E-I-E-I-O.

Open, Shut Them

Open, shut them, open, shut them,
    give a little clap.
Open, shut them, open, shut them,
    lay them in your lap.
Creep them, creep them, creep them,
    creep them right up to your chin.
Open wide your little mouth, but do not let
    them in.

Pat-a-Cake

Pat-a-cake, pat-a-cake, baker's man,

Bake me a cake as fast as you can.

Pat it and roll it and mark it with a B,

And put it in the oven for baby and me.

Pease Porridge Hot

Pease porridge hot, pease porridge cold,

Pease porridge in the pot, nine days old.

Some like it hot, some like it cold,

Some like it in the pot, nine days old.

Pop Goes the Weasel

Round and 'round the mulberry bush

The monkey chased the weasel.

The monkey thought 'twas all in fun.

Pop goes the weasel.

67

Ring Around the Rosy

Ring around the rosy,
A pocket full of posies.
Ashes, ashes,
We all fall down.

Rock-a-Bye Baby

Rock-a-bye baby, in the tree top,

When the wind blows, the cradle will rock.

When the bough breaks, the cradle will fall,

And down will come baby, cradle, and all.

Row, Row, Row Your Boat

Row, row, row your boat
Gently down the stream.
Merrily, merrily, merrily, merrily,
Life is but a dream.

Rub-a-dub-dub

Rub-a-dub-dub, three men in a tub,

And who do you think they be?

The butcher, the baker,

the candlestick maker.

Turn them out, knaves all three.

See Saw, Margery Daw

See saw, Margery Daw,

Johnny shall have a new master.

He shall have but a penny a day

because he can't work any faster.

Shoe the Horse

Shoe the horse, shoe the horse,

Shoe the bay mare.

Here a nail, there a nail,

Still she stands there.

Sing a Song of Sixpence

Sing a song of sixpence, a pocket full of rye.

Four and twenty blackbirds baked in a pie.

When the pie was opened

    the birds began to sing.

Wasn't that a dainty dish to set before the king?

Swing Our Hands

Swing our hands, swing our hands,
swing our hands together.

Swing our hands, swing our hands,
in our circle now.
Tap our toes, tap our toes,
tap our toes together.
Tap our toes, tap our toes,
in our circle now.

Teddy Bear

Teddy bear, teddy bear, turn around,

Teddy bear, teddy bear, touch the ground.

Teddy bear, teddy bear, show your shoe,

Teddy bear, teddy bear, that will do!

There Was a Duke of York

There was a duke of York.

He had ten thousand men.

He marched them up the hill.

And then he marched them down again.

When you're up, you're up.

And when you're down, you're down.

And when you're only halfway up

You're neither up nor down.

This Is the Way We Wash Our Clothes

This is the way we wash our clothes,

wash our clothes, wash our clothes.

This is the way we wash our clothes,

so early in the morning.

83

This Little Piggy

This little piggy went to market,
 and this little piggy stayed home;
This little piggy had roast beef,
 and this little piggy had none;
And this little piggy cried,
 Wee, wee, wee, all the way home.

Twinkle, Twinkle, Little Star

Twinkle, twinkle, little star.

How I wonder what you are.

Up above the world so high,

Like a diamond in the sky.

Twinkle, twinkle, little star

How I wonder what you are.

Wheels on the Bus

The wheels on the bus go round and round,
 round and round, round and round.
The wheels on the bus go round and round
 all through the town.
The baby on the bus goes, Wah wah wah,
 wah wah wah, wah wah wah.
The baby on the bus goes Wah wah wah,
 all through the town.
The lights on the bus go blink blink blink,
 blink blink blink, blink blink blink,
The light on the bus go blink blink blink,
 all through the town.

The driver on the bus says,

"Move on back, move on back, move on back,"

The driver on the bus says,

"Move on back," all through the town.

The money on the bus goes, clink clink clink,

   clink clink clink, clink clink clink,

The money on the bus goes, clink clink clink,

   all through the town.

The people on the bus go up and down,
up and down, up and down,
The people on the bus go up and down,
all through the town.

The wipers on the bus go, swish swish swish,

swish swish swish, swish swish swish,

The wipers on the bus go, swish swish swish,

all through the town.

Where Is Thumbkin?

Where is Thumbkin?

Where is Thumbkin?

Here I am, here I am.

How are you today, sir?

Very well, I thank you.

Run away, run away.

Where, Oh Where Is Pretty Little Susie?

Where, oh where is pretty little Susie?

Where, oh where is pretty little Susie?

Where, oh where is pretty little Susie?

Way down yonder in the pawpaw patch.

Yankee Doodle

Oh, Yankee Doodle went to town,
  a-riding on a pony;
He stuck a feather in his cap
  and called it macaroni.
Yankee Doodle keep it up;
  Yankee Doodle Dandy,
Mind the music and the step,
  and with the girls be handy.